This book belongs to:

_____

Digital art by Callaway Animation Studios under the direction of David Kirk in collaboration with Nelvana Limited.

This book is based on the TV episode "Top o' Big Tree," written by Scott Kraft, from the animated TV series *Miss Spider's Sunny Patch Friends* on Nick Jr., a Nelvana Limited/Absolute Pictures Limited co-production in association with Callaway Arts & Entertainment, based on the Miss Spider books by David Kirk.

Nicholas Callaway, President and Publisher
Cathy Ferrara, Managing Editor and Production Director
Toshiya Masuda, Art Director • Nelson Gomez, Director of Digital Services
Joya Rajadhyaksha, Associate Editor • Amy Cloud, Associate Editor
Bill Burg, Digital Artist • Keith McMenamy, Digital Artist • Christina Pagano, Digital Artist
Raphael Shea, Art Assistant • Krupa Jhaveri, Design Assistant

Special thanks to the Nelvana staff, including Doug Murphy, Scott Dyer, Tracy Ewing, Pam Lehn,
Tonya Lindo, Mark Picard, Susie Grondin, Luis Lopez, Eric Pentz, and Georgina Robinson.

Library of Congress Cataloging-in-Publication Data available upon request.

Distributed in the United States by Penguin Young Readers Group.

Callaway Arts & Entertainment, its Callaway logotype,
and Callaway & Kirk Company LLC are trademarks.

ISBN 978-0-448-45010-0

Visit Callaway Arts & Entertainment at www.callaway.com.

10 9 8 7 6 5 4 3 2 1   08 09 10

Printed in China

Top o' Big Tree

David Kirk

CALLAWAY

NEW YORK

2008

The Sunny Patch bug scouts were having a meeting.

Mr. Mantis said, "Tomorrow is our hike up the big tulip tree."

"That's the tallest tree in Sunny Patch!" Snowdrop said nervously.

"But if we reach the top," Squirt told her, "we will get our bug scout wings!"

The next morning, Mr. Mantis limped into the Cozy Hole with a sprained thorax.

"I'm afraid we'll have to put off our climb," he sighed.

The little bug scouts were so disappointed!

Mr. Mantis asked Miss Spider to lead them.

"I'm coaching Dragon's basketberry team today," said Miss Spider.

"Then perhaps Holley?" asked Mr. Mantis.

"I've never been camping before," Holley said nervously, "but I could try."

With Holley as their guide, Bounce and Squirt raced ahead.

"Hold your horseflies!" Holley cried. "If you rush, you'll miss all the wonderful sights."

"Yes," Snowdrop agreed. "This branch's rings show that the tree is very old."

"Time for a snack!" Holley announced after a bit more climbing. "These tulip tree flowers are delicious!"

The scouts kept climbing. The sky grew dim, and they stopped for the night. Pansy and Bounce started dinner.

"I'll hang our sleeping sacs," Squirt said.

"Wow, you bugs sure know your camping lessons!" Holley beamed proudly.

The stars looked brighter from high in the tree.

"Look! There's the bug dipper!" Squirt cried.

Soon the little bugs closed their weary eyes, falling asleep under the twinkling sky.

The next morning, Squirt and Bounce felt very sore.

"Maybe we climbed too fast yesterday," Holley said.

"I don't know if I can make it to the top of the tree," Bounce moaned.

"Climbing Big Tree is a lot harder than I thought," Squirt panted.

"Come on, kids," Holley said. "I know we can do it!"

Finally, Squirt and Bounce were too tired to go any further.

"Snowdrop, you and Dad keep going," Squirt sighed. "At least one of us should get bug scout wings."

"No way," Snowdrop insisted. "Bug scouts stick together."

"Why don't we stash our packs in this hole?" Holley suggested. "It would be easier to climb without them."

After putting down their packs, Squirt said, "I'm sure I can get to the top now!"

"We are *s-so* high," Snowdrop stammered. "I'm scared!"

"You can do it, Snowdrop," Squirt said, helping her up. "Bugs scouts stick together, remember?"

"We'll *all* be first to the top," panted Bounce.

Finally, the travelers
reached the very tip of
the highest branch.

"Great job!" Holley smiled,
awarding each bug a pair
of wings.

"But Dad,"
said Snowdrop,
"You should have
a pair of wings, too!"

Snowdrop had the honor of pinning wings on the newest scout in Sunny Patch.

Atop the tree, the happy campers cheered.